Airship Adventure

Written by
Cath Jones

Illustrated by
Alessandro D'urso

Chapter 1

Sami tightened her tool belt and strode across the aerodrome. She paused for a moment by the mooring mast to admire her mother's airship. The morning sunshine sparkled on the brass propellers and a flutter of anticipation rose within her. She could hardly wait to see the airship *Victory* fly. Would Mum's invention really work as well as everyone expected? Would they win the contest?

"Sami!" called a voice.

She grinned at the sight of her best friend, Amrit. She waved back at him as he finished polishing one of the *Victory's* propellers.

Airship Adventure

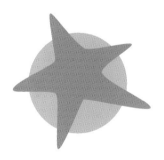

'Airship Adventure'
An original concept by Cath Jones
© Cath Jones 2022

Illustrated by Alessandro D'urso

Published by MAVERICK ARTS PUBLISHING LTD
Studio 11, City Business Centre, 6 Brighton Road,
Horsham, West Sussex, RH13 5BB
© Maverick Arts Publishing Limited August 2022
+44 (0)1403 256941

A CIP catalogue record for this book is available at the British Library.

ISBN 978-1-84886-916-5

www.maverickbooks.co.uk

This book is rated as: Grey Band (Guided Reading)

"Hurry up!" Amrit shouted, his face crinkling into a happy smile. "There's loads to finish before tomorrow's flight!"

A pigeon fluttered onto a nearby oak tree before darting into the airship. With a jolt of delight, Sami spotted a tiny tube fixed to its leg. This was the messenger pigeon they'd all been waiting for! She raced after it, her feet thundering on the ironwork of the spiral staircase.

"Mum!" she yelled, "it's here!" Her voice echoed

around the airship.

Alarmed by Sami's shouts, the pigeon took flight and zoomed into the cabin. Excitement fizzed through Sami as she skidded after it.

Emerald Cooper, Sami's mum, turned in surprise. "Samantha! What's all this commotion for?" Her brow furrowed in concern.

Sami huffed loudly. She was only called 'Samantha' when she was in trouble. She pointed at the bird. "The messenger pigeon's arrived!"

A hush fell over the cabin as all the crew members gazed expectantly at Emerald.

Sami cupped her hands together and the pigeon hopped on, nestling in comfortably. She offered the bird to her mum.

Emerald shook her head. "You read the message, Sami."

Sami's hands trembled with excitement as she unclipped the tube. "It's from the queen," she said, pointing at the royal crest.

Wishing you the best of luck in Friday's Royal Postal Contest. The Post Master General will deliver test letters to all participants later today. The first one to deliver the test letter to the palace before 8pm on Friday will be granted the Royal Postal Warrant.

As excited chatter broke out, Sami wondered for a moment who else would be competing for the royal warrant.

Emerald held up a hand for silence. "I am confident that, by 8pm on Friday, we will have won the Royal Postal Warrant. The *Victory* will become the main method of transport for the Royal Postal Service."

Everyone cheered.

Sami and Amrit carried the pigeon outside and watched it fly away. "Are you nervous?" Amrit asked.

"Should I be?"

"Well, your mum's airship is a ground-breaking new invention and..." He shrugged and his voice trailed off. Sami raised her eyebrows questioningly. "...I've heard rumours. Some people don't like change. They're used to messenger pigeons..."

Sami snorted loudly. "The *Victory* is progress! Think how many messages and parcels she'll be able to carry. No more messages going missing because a bird doesn't arrive."

"I'm just saying, maybe we should stay alert. What if some of the pigeon owners decide they want to stop the

Victory winning the Royal Warrant?"

Sami jumped up. "If anybody wants to try any funny business, I'll be waiting."

"*We'll* be waiting!" Amrit said.

They climbed up onto the top of the departure platform. It was the perfect place to keep watch. Sami peered through her vision-a-scope. If anyone was planning to

sabotage the *Victory*, she would see them coming.

Silence settled over the aerodrome as they watched the sun set.

Suddenly, Sami tensed.

"What?" Amrit whispered.

"Shh!" she hissed. "I can hear ticking." She gestured towards the perimeter fence.

"Ticking!" squeaked Amrit in alarm. "Do you think someone's going to try and blow up the *Victory*?"

Chapter 2

Tick tock, tick tock, tick tock.

Sami and Amrit crept towards the sound.

Just outside the perimeter fence, a cloaked figure was crouched down next to a strange-looking penny-farthing bicycle. He held a large winding key in gloved hands.

Tick tock, tick tock, tick tock.

"It must be a clockwork penny-farthing!" Sami whispered. "I've never heard of one of those before. Come on, I want to get a better look."

They edged closer.

The man's black top hat was tipped forward, shadowing his face. Sami frowned. Suddenly, the man stood up and started to mutter to himself! "A ship in the sky! No, no, no! The sky is for birds. It needs to be stopped..."

CRASH!

The muttering ceased and the man froze. His eyes searched the darkness.

Amrit stared in shock at a bucket he'd just accidentally kicked over.

"Duck!" whispered Sami.

But it was too late. The shadowy figure stared straight at Sami! Quick as a flash, he leapt onto the clockwork contraption. Sami watched in horror as the penny-farthing and the mysterious stranger zoomed away into the darkness, accompanied by the sound of speedy tick-tocking.

"After him!" yelled Sami.

But the stranger vanished round a bend and they lost sight of him.

"We're never going to catch up with something clockwork," Amrit moaned.

"Just keep running!" Sami urged.

After a few minutes, Amrit slowed. They had reached the edge of a dark wood. He leant against a large oak tree, clutched his side and groaned. "I can't run any further. I've got a stitch."

Sami peered for a moment at the oak tree. A poster advertising a circus was nailed onto it. She gazed into the darkness and sighed. "We'll never find him in here."

An owl hooted, as if agreeing.

"I can't help feeling that we're being watched," Amrit muttered anxiously.

"We *are* being watched. Look!" Sami pointed up into the branches of a nearby tree. "Pigeons!" she said with a quiet laugh.

The pigeons cooed quietly at them.

"I think we should get back to the aerodrome," Amrit said uneasily.

"Good idea." As she turned, Sami's foot scuffed something on the ground.

"What is it?" Amrit asked.

"Some kind of notebook." Sami fanned the pages, scanning them quickly. "It's got lots of drawings in it."

She let out a low whistle and held out a page for Amrit to see. "These drawings are beautiful. Look at the detail in the sketches of birds."

"Are there only drawings of pigeons?" Amrit asked.

"Yes, I think so," Sami said, nodding slowly.

"That's a bit weird. I mean, it's not a very exciting bird to choose, is it?"

Sami shrugged. "Look, the back of the notebook is

filled with diagrams." One diagram in particular caught her eye. "This one is crazy-looking."

"Are those wings?" Amrit asked.

"Yep. I think it's a design for some sort of invention; it looks like a mechanical bird!"

"So it's a flying machine?"

Sami nodded. "But not like my mum's airship. I think this would be much smaller. For one person maybe?"

Amrit looked thoughtful. "I think we should show this notebook to your mum."

As they neared the aerodrome, Sami sniffed. "Can you smell smoke?" she asked.

Amrit pointed at puffs of steam rising into the air.

Sami peered through her vision-a-scope and let out an excited whoop. "It's the Postmaster General's steam-a-wheel. It must be the test letter!"

The steam-a-wheel vehicle trundled through the gates of the aerodrome, steam billowing from its two funnels. Two bright lights attached to its front were like gleaming eyes, staring into the darkness.

"Come on, I don't want to miss this!" Sami said.

Chapter 3

By the time Sami and Amrit reached the *Victory*, Emerald was already standing in front of the steam-a-wheel. The Post Master General climbed out and tipped her top hat. She pulled out an envelope. Sami and Amrit could only watch from a distance as the letter was handed over. The airship's crew and ground staff clapped enthusiastically.

"Mum looks busy," Sami said. "I don't think we should bother her right now."

"But..." Amrit hesitated.

Sami turned the pages of the notebook and studied the intricate diagram of the giant mechanical bird. She traced a series of cogs with her finger.

"Back in those wood, did you notice a circus poster on a tree?" she asked.

"Yeah. Why?"

"I'm sure the circus poster had a mechanical bird on it just like this one. I think there's a connection between the circus and that stranger."

"So?"

"There's a performance later tonight. I think we should go."

Doubt flashed across Amrit's face. "Really?"

"You heard Penny-farthing Man muttering about stopping the airship. Well, I reckon this is his notebook. If he and his mechanical bird are performing tonight, I want to talk to him."

"Oh!" Amrit swallowed nervously. "I was afraid you were going to say that."

The circus big top was surrounded by shabby-looking steam homes. One had been divided into multiple sections. Each section housed a pigeon. They cooed quietly as Sami and Amrit approached.

"Messenger pigeons!" Sami mouthed.

The sound of trumpets drifted from inside the big top.

Amrit tugged on her sleeve. "I think the show's starting."

They perched at the back of the wooden seating area. Sami wished people would take off their top hats when they sat down. "Tall people and top hats shouldn't be allowed," she muttered darkly.

The first act was a young man who conjured pigeons from a top hat. Next came a clockwork robot wearing a sequinned tutu. She persuaded pigeons to soar in and out of hoops. Finally, the ringmaster tipped his silver top hat and announced that they would be dazzled and amazed by Birdman!

Sami leant forward,
not wanting to miss anything.

The lights dropped. Puffs of smoke
wafted into the ring and mysterious music
played. Then a giant mechanical bird soared into the
ring! There was a goggled figure sitting *inside* the bird,
controlling the wings.

Sami's mouth hung open in wonder. The audience
gasped as a flock of pigeons flew into the ring and raced
round with him. It was a breathtaking performance.

Afterwards, Sami felt exhausted. "Wow," she murmured.

"Did you hear that?" Amrit asked.

"No, what?"

"The woman sitting in front of us said that all the birds in the circus are retired messenger birds," Amrit said. "Don't you think that's a funny kind of circus?"

Sami shrugged. "Maybe. But I think we should talk to Birdman," she said in an urgent whisper.

As the big top emptied, they followed a crowd of admirers backstage. Birdman was bowing his appreciation to the delighted onlookers. Sami waved and he flapped his clockwork wings, lifting off the ground for a moment.

"Did you enjoy my show?" he asked.

"Your mechanical bird is a remarkable invention," Sami said.

"Thank you, I..." he paused mid-sentence.

Behind his goggles, Sami saw his grey eyes narrow. She almost shivered; his stare was ice cold.

Suddenly, he jabbed a finger at the airship brooch on her coat.

"The Airship *Victory*!" he spat.

"My mother's airship…" Sami began.

"I think this conversation is over," interrupted Birdman. He scowled furiously, then flapped his wings and swooped away into the night.

Chapter 4

Sami woke early the next morning. A dazzling sunrise greeted her gaze. It was perfect weather for the maiden flight of the *Victory*. There was hardly a breath of wind in a cloudless sky.

She hurried into the cabin, feeling a flush of pride at the sight of her mother wearing a captain's hat. Should she tell her about the notebook and Birdman when she was so very busy?

Emerald beamed happily when she spotted Sami. "Sami! Where have you been?"

Now's my chance to tell her, Sami thought. But, before she could say anything, her mum held out the test letter.

Sami stared in confusion.

"I would like you to take charge of this."

"What?" Sami gasped.

"Guard it with utmost care!"

"Of course!" Her mother had invested all her money into this airship. If they failed to deliver the test letter, they would be ruined. She felt weak as she tucked the letter into the chest pocket of her jacket. To be trusted with such an important task!

Emerald checked her pocket watch. "Ladies and gentlemen, this is Captain Emerald Cooper..." she called in a commanding voice. "Please put on your goggles to protect your eyes from the rays of the sun as we rise high up into the air."

Dozens of tickets had been sold for this maiden voyage and the gangway was packed with people.

Sami felt a flutter of excitement in her chest as she put on the leather-rimmed goggles. The thick, tinted glass turned the world slightly orange.

Emerald spoke instructions into a brass communication tube. Sami pictured the engineer checking instruments and flicking switches.

The cabin flight crew began to wind ornate brass handles. Hinged flaps unfolded on the exterior of the ship, revealing banks of mirrors.

There were gasps of amazement from the passengers.

Emerald held up her hand for silence. "In a moment, this historic voyage will commence. When the rays of the sun land on the mirrors, the heat will be amplified and directed into huge tanks of water. The water will turn to steam and pipes will funnel this energy directly to the power room. There, the heat will provide energy to turn a series of cogs to propel the ship."

She checked her pocket watch again. "Only ten seconds left before the contest begins!" She gestured to the linesman on the runway. As the tethers fell away from the airship, the nose swung round to face the sun. Seconds later, pistons began to pump and propellers turned.

"Release the weights," ordered Emerald.

The airship began to rise. The whirring of the propellers formed into a steady rhythmic thrum. Sami stared out of the windows and noticed rows of pigeons perched on the perimeter fence. Her stomach twisted anxiously. Should she have told Mum about Birdman?

She and Amrit spent the next few hours on the observation deck, staring out in wonder. Sami stayed alert for any sign of Birdman.

"There's no sign of any of the other competitors," Amrit said. "Do you think we're in the lead?"

Sami nodded. "I think we might be. We overtook a couple of flying machines soon after we took off. And I heard someone saying at least one machine has made an emergency landing. I don't think there can be many entrants still flying."

Behind them, clockwork waiter-robots circulated with silver trays bearing ornate crystal glasses of bubbling drinks. Their quiet tick-tocking was lost amidst the excited laughter of the passengers and crew. Cries of delight went up when the royal palace was finally sighted in the far distance.

As the sun began to set, the *Victory* switched to clockwork power. Everything was going exactly according to plan. Sami tried to push away the nagging feeling of worry.

Suddenly, dazzling beams of light lit up the airship.

"Searchlights!" said Amrit in surprise. "I wonder what they're looking for?"

Sami's heart sank. "Us?" she whispered.

Chapter 5

Sami pointed to where the searchlights were coming from: the top of a nearby hill. A giant clockwork mechanism was positioned next to a strange-looking contraption.

"What's that?" she asked.

Amrit gulped nervously. "That looks like a giant catapult!"

As they watched, a series of cogs began to move, which in turn drove round a thick metal chain. This pulled a large band which was stretched between the struts of the catapult.

"I think it's preparing to fire!" Sami murmured.

Suddenly, there was a loud **crack.**

Sami flinched. "Look!"

Something had been fired into the sky.

"It's Birdman!" Amrit yelled.

Everyone gazed in shock. "Birdman?" they repeated in puzzled voices.

The catapult launched Birdman and his mechanical bird into the air at great speed. He soared through the sky, wings spread wide. It took only seconds for him to reach the same height as the *Victory*. His huge mechanical wings flapped rapidly.

"What is that?" Emerald asked in an alarmed voice.

"That's Birdman," Sami said.

"And he doesn't like airships..." Amrit added.

Birdman was not alone. An enormous flock of pigeons swooped and darted around him, riding the sky breezes.

A sense of hopelessness slipped over Sami. Why, oh, why hadn't she told Mum everything?

Birdman swooped in close to the cabin.

"What's that by his mouth?" Amrit asked. But he didn't need to wait long to find out.

"Turn back," ordered a loud mechanical voice.

"He's got a voice-amplifier," Sami said. She'd seen it in the notebook.

Emerald flicked a brass switch and the speakers on board the *Victory* crackled into life. "We intend to deliver the test letter to the palace. Please stay clear of our flight path."

Birdman soared backwards and forwards in front of the windows of the cabin. "The sky belongs to my birds, not airships," he said through his voice-amplifier. "Generations of my family have provided messenger

pigeons to the postal service. We have ensured the safe arrival of millions of messages."

"He must be taking part in the postal contest too," Amrit whispered to Sami.

Sami watched the mechanical bird gliding effortlessly on the wind, transfixed by the elegant flaps of its clockwork wings. Her mind turned to the diagram in the notebook. She couldn't help but wonder what the clockwork mechanism was made of? Surely metal cogs would be too heavy to fly?

In response to Birdman's words, Emerald turned the *Victory's* huge, wooden steering wheel. Immediately, the mechanical bird changed course too. With effortless ease, it gained on the *Victory*. Then the pigeons swarmed around the airship and began to peck! They were attacking the *Victory*!

Sami watched helplessly as the airship manoeuvred slowly this way and that, trying to avoid the stab of the birds' beaks. She put her hands over her ears. The noise of ripping material and cracking support struts was terrible. She pulled her jacket close to her chest, feeling the test letter safe inside.

Suddenly, the floor of the *Victory* tilted beneath Sami's feet. She stumbled against a window, her face pressed up against the cold glass. The airship was in trouble! They began to lose height, sinking lower and lower. Soon, it had lost so much height, Sami could clearly see the faces of people staring up from the bridge below.

Amrit pointed in alarm. "We're going to hit that bridge!"

Sami gasped as Birdman swooped past. He was so close; she could almost hear the wind whistling through the cloth on his mechanical wings. His face was hidden behind an enormous pair of tinted goggles.

Amrit dropped onto his knees and grabbed Sami's hand. "We're going to crash!"

Chapter 6

The *Victory's* internal transmitters crackled into life. Once again, the airship was filled with the sound of Emerald's voice. "We must gain height. All hands on deck to lighten our load."

"Help me ditch the stabiliser sand," Sami urged Amrit. She pulled out a handle tucked beneath a window and began to turn it. There was a gentle thud as a flap opened on the outside of the airship. Sand began to stream into the air.

Amrit dashed to the opposite side of the ship and did the same. They raced from window to window, frantically turning handles.

"Is it working?" Amrit panted.

There was a soft thump as the *Victory* bumped across the top of the bridge.

"We're gaining height!" Sami yelled.

The faces of the boaters on the river below began to fade from view. But with the stabiliser sand ditched, the *Victory* rocked from side to side in an alarming manner. Sami and Amrit staggered through the airship and flung themselves into the cabin.

Emerald stared straight ahead, her hands tightly gripping the airship's steering wheel. "Well done on releasing the stabiliser sand," she murmured in a calm voice. "Prepare to land in five minutes."

"What?" Sami rushed to the window and hope flared within her. There was the royal palace. Its lights glittered out of the darkness. "We're almost there!" she whispered.

Amrit pointed. "So is Birdman."

The *Victory* landed in a park directly opposite the palace. Sami threw open an emergency escape hatch and hurled out two rope ladders. As the crew of the Victory streamed down onto the grass, Birdman landed too. He pushed a pair of chunky goggles off his face and glared at the airship.

Sami stared in surprise. She had expected someone younger... she wasn't sure why.

"Who are you?!" demanded Emerald.

"John Montgomery-Smyth." He bowed his head slightly.

"Commonly known as Birdman," Sami added.

"You attacked us! You tried to drive us out of the sky." Emerald's voice shook with anger.

"Ah..." he paused for a moment. "My apologies. That was unintentional. My birds got carried away. I was merely trying to delay you."

"But why?" Sami interrupted.

Emerald snorted loudly. "He's a cheat, that's why. So desperate to win the Royal Postal Warrant..."

"Your airship is stealing my son's future!" Birdman interrupted. Anger flared in his voice. "When I was a boy,

I helped my grandfather tend his messenger pigeons. When he retired, my father took over and then I too worked for the postal service with our birds..."

"My airships *are* the future!" Emerald declared. "You can't stop progress."

"Yes I can! Especially if you fail to deliver your test letter, and I deliver mine."

Emerald flicked open her pocket watch. "Well I hope you're satisfied. It appears that we have *both* run out of time."

Sami's mind whirled. "It's not eight o'clock yet. There's still five minutes left. We could work together."

"Together?" Birdman looked scornful.

"Your mechanical bird is as amazing an invention as my mum's airship. It would be great for delivering smaller packages. Mum's airship could deliver bigger parcels over longer distances. Your son's messenger pigeons would be perfect for letters."

Uncertainty flickered across Birdman's face.

"We can be a team." Sami added. She pulled out the test letter. "We could deliver our letters together. There's still time."

Emerald smiled. "I believe my daughter has come up with a rather sensible plan..."

Sami glowed with pride at her mother's words. She held out her hand. "Do we have an agreement?"

Birdman nodded and suddenly smiled.

Sami, Emerald and Birdman shook hands.

Across the road, the royal clock began to whirr into life. It was about to strike eight!

"Hurry! We've only seconds left," Sami cried.

Emerald, Sami and Amrit ran. Birdman swooped into the air.

As they raced through the palace gates, Sami spotted the Post Master General waiting in front of the palace letterbox.

BONG! The clock began to strike.

Sami sprinted the last few metres. Just behind them, Birdman touched down. Together, they placed their test letters into the hands of the Post Master General.

They'd done it! Now Birdman and his son's messenger pigeons could continue to deliver messages and the *Victory* would be part of the Royal Postal Service too!

Discussion Points

1. Who is the captain of the *Victory*?

2. What do Sami and Amrit find in the woods after chasing the man on the penny-farthing?

a) A notebook full of bird sketches and inventions

b) A wheel from the bicycle

c) A strange machine

3. What was your favourite part of the story?

4. Where do Sami and Amrit first see Birdman?

5. Why do you think Birdman wanted to stop the *Victory* from winning the competition?

6. Who was your favourite character and why?

7. There were moments in the story when the characters had to **compromise**. Where do you think the story shows this most?

8. What do you think happens after the end of the story?

Book Bands for Guided Reading

Pink
Red
Yellow
Blue
Green
Orange
Turquoise
Purple
Gold
White
Lime
Brown
Grey

The Institute of Education book banding system is a scale of colours that reflects the various levels of reading difficulty. The bands are assigned by taking into account the content, the language style, the layout and phonics. Word, phrase and sentence level work is also taken into consideration.

The Maverick Readers Scheme is a bright, attractive range of books covering the pink to grey bands. All of these books have been book banded for guided reading to the industry standard and edited by a leading educational consultant.

To view the whole Maverick Readers scheme, visit our website at

www.maverickearlyreaders.com

Or scan the QR code to view our scheme instantly!

Maverick Chapter Readers
(From Lime to Grey Band)